Broken

Johnny Gee

Published by Golden Ember Edition, 2024.

BROKEN

First edition. November 22, 2024.

ISBN: 979-8230625643

Written by Johnny Gee.

Table of Contents

Chapter 1: The Weight of Independence

Moving into my first apartment was supposed to be monumental. A turning point. A triumphant leap into adulthood, complete with bills, questionable furniture, and the lingering smell of someone else's life. The key had barely turned in the lock when I realized I had no idea what I was doing. The place was empty, in that aggressively indifferent way that only rental apartments can achieve. The walls were beige. The carpet was a colorless gray that seemed to exist solely to hide stains. And the air? It carried the faint scent of onions, despite the glaring absence of any onions.

Still, this was mine. My space. My sanctuary. My problem.

The boxes arrived a few hours after I did, shoved into the entryway by a delivery guy who clearly wanted to be anywhere else. I tipped him out of obligation, not generosity, and immediately regretted it. I hadn't even opened the first box and I was already hemorrhaging money. I told myself that was just part of the deal—adulthood was expensive, and so was pretending to be good at it.

The first box contained books. That part made sense. Books were a safe start, heavy but manageable, and easy to stack. The second box contained kitchen utensils, though I couldn't remember packing half of them. Did I own a whisk? Apparently, I did. Or I had stolen one during the moving process, which seemed unlikely. I was the kind of person who paid for extra sauce packets at fast food joints to avoid judgment, so theft wasn't really in my wheelhouse.

By the time I'd emptied the third box, the apartment was still far too empty. There was a chair in the corner—a relic from my parents' basement—and a small table I'd picked up from a garage sale. It wobbled slightly, which felt appropriate. Everything wobbled now. My life, my bank account, my confidence—it was all a little off-balance.

The ritual of unpacking became a way to stave off the silence. Every item I placed felt like an attempt to ground myself, to say, This is home now. I lined my books up alphabetically because it seemed like the sort of thing a person who had their life together might do. I folded my clothes and placed them into drawers with the precision of a surgeon, even though half of them were thrift store finds with mysterious stains.

Still, no matter how many items I unpacked, the space felt wrong. Too open, too quiet, too...waiting.

I spent the first night trying to ignore the sound of the refrigerator. It wasn't loud, exactly, but it had a way of humming at the wrong frequency, a persistent reminder that I wasn't alone in the apartment. Not in the comforting, roommate kind of way, but in the way that made me wonder if the building itself was watching. The hum would stop just long enough for me to think it was gone, only to return with a vengeance the moment my guard dropped.

I tried to distract myself with the glow of my phone screen. Social media was a black hole I willingly threw myself into, even though I knew it would only make me feel worse. Pictures of smiling faces, curated lives, people posing with friends, significant others, pets, and jobs that probably came with health insurance. I scrolled until my thumb hurt, then locked the phone and stared at the ceiling. It was cracked in a way that almost looked deliberate, like the building had been designed to remind tenants of their fragility.

It was around midnight when the thought hit me: I'd left something behind. Not a box, not a piece of furniture—something else. Something intangible and essential, like the piece of a puzzle that makes the rest of the picture make sense. The more I tried to pin it down, the more elusive it became. It wasn't loneliness, though loneliness was certainly making itself at home. It wasn't regret, though that was hovering just outside the door, waiting for an invitation.

It was a weight I couldn't name, pressing on my chest like an anchor tethered to nowhere.

The morning came too soon, accompanied by the unforgiving light of a single window that refused to close properly. I stumbled into the kitchen, where the fridge greeted me with its usual hum of existential indifference. The coffee maker was a cheap model that spat out a lukewarm approximation of coffee, which I sipped anyway because caffeine was caffeine.

The day stretched ahead of me, empty and waiting. There was no schedule to follow, no boss to answer to, no family hovering over my shoulder. This was freedom, I told myself. This was what I'd wanted. So why did it feel like failure?

I busied myself with tasks that felt important but weren't—straightening the books I'd already aligned, rearranging the contents of drawers, counting the tiles in the bathroom. Eighteen. There were eighteen tiles, not including the ones behind the toilet, which seemed unfairly difficult to reach. I cleaned them anyway, scrubbing with the fervor of someone trying to erase more than just dirt.

By the afternoon, I'd exhausted every reasonable excuse to stay inside. The fridge was stocked, the furniture was arranged, and the tile grout was cleaner than it had any right to be. The thought of leaving the apartment was both thrilling and terrifying, so I compromised by standing in the doorway for ten minutes, staring at the hallway like it might bite.

When I finally stepped out, the air felt wrong—thicker somehow, heavier. The hallway was empty, lined with identical doors that gave no indication of the lives hidden behind them. I made it to the elevator without incident, though I kept glancing over my shoulder like someone might be following. The elevator ride down was mercifully short, though it creaked in a way that suggested it might one day become very, very long.

The world outside the building was bright and loud, full of people who seemed entirely too certain of their direction. I wandered aimlessly, letting the city guide me, though it felt less like guidance and more like being herded. The streets were crowded but impersonal, full of faces I wouldn't remember and who wouldn't remember me. That was comforting, in a way. I could disappear here, and no one would notice.

By the time I returned to the apartment, the weight on my chest had only grown heavier. The fridge greeted me like an old friend, humming its song of indifference as I collapsed into the chair. The unpacked boxes sat in the corner, waiting for me to deal with them. I ignored them, staring instead at the window that refused to close. The breeze it let in was cool and sharp, like it belonged to a world that wasn't mine.

As the evening stretched into night, I let my mind wander. The thought returned—the sense that I'd left something behind, something I couldn't name. I tried to shake it off, to convince myself it was just the adjustment period, the growing pains of independence. But the feeling lingered, heavy and immovable, as though it had claimed the space as its own.

I stared at the ceiling until the cracks blurred together, until the fridge's hum became white noise, until the weight in my chest felt like it had always been there.

The first day was over. It hadn't been monumental. It hadn't even been particularly good. But it was mine, and that was supposed to be enough.

Right?

Chapter 2: First Steps into Routine

Starting a new job feels like stepping onto a stage without a script. You know the scene, you understand the premise, but the lines? Completely up to improvisation. For me, that meant walking into the building with an expression I hoped conveyed confidence but probably looked more like a cat that had just been scolded for knocking over a glass.

The office was dimly lit, as though the overhead lights were saving their full wattage for more deserving spaces. Cubicles stretched out like a labyrinth, the beige walls offering all the charm of a waiting room. My desk was in the corner, close to a buzzing fluorescent light that flickered just often enough to be maddening. I took it as a sign that this was where I belonged.

I'd practiced smiling in the mirror before coming here. Not too much teeth, not too forced—just enough to say, Yes, I'm competent, and no, I'm not plotting your demise. It had felt rehearsed then, but it felt downright fraudulent now, especially as my new manager, Susan, explained my duties with the enthusiasm of a brick.

"This is your workstation," she said, gesturing to the desk with a clipboard in hand. "You'll handle data entry, filing, and the occasional phone call. Simple stuff."

"Simple," I echoed, nodding. Simple was good. Simple was manageable. Simple wouldn't crush me like a beetle under a boot.

Susan didn't seem convinced. She tilted her head like she was trying to figure out if I was actually listening or just nodding on autopilot. The answer, of course, was both.

The day passed in a haze of clicking keyboards, shuffling papers, and the occasional cough from a coworker whose cubicle was just far enough away to be anonymous. My tasks weren't complicated, but they required focus, and focus meant silencing the running commentary in my head.

I masked, as I always did. It was an art I'd honed over years—mirroring the tone of whoever spoke to me, adopting the gestures and phrases that seemed to fit the situation. When Susan asked if everything was going okay, I nodded and said, "Absolutely," with the same cadence she used. It was exhausting, but it worked. People saw what they wanted to see: someone competent, someone normal.

I counted things to stay grounded. The steps it took to walk from my desk to the breakroom (thirteen). The number of clicks it took to close a browser window (four). The number of breaths I took in a minute (seventeen, though that one fluctuated).

At lunch, I ate alone in the corner of the breakroom, trying not to look like someone eating alone in the corner of the breakroom. I pulled out my phone and scrolled through a news feed that felt like a collage of bad decisions and worse outcomes. A coworker glanced my way once, then immediately turned back to their sandwich. I wasn't sure if I was relieved or offended.

By the time the day ended, I felt like a wrung-out dishcloth. I left the building with my bag slung over one shoulder, my steps steady and deliberate. I counted them, as always, marking the rhythm like a metronome: one, two, three, four. Five. Six.

The city looked different at night. The neon signs flickered with a kind of desperation, their lights casting long shadows that stretched across the pavement. People moved quickly, heads down, as though the dark made them eager to reach anywhere but here.

I felt watched.

It wasn't a conscious thought at first—more of a creeping awareness, like the prickling sensation you get when a spider is somewhere nearby, just out of sight. I glanced over my shoulder. Nothing. Just an empty stretch of sidewalk illuminated by the dull orange glow of a streetlight. I kept walking.

The feeling didn't go away. Every step seemed louder, the echo of my boots against the pavement magnified in the silence. My shadow stretched long and thin in front of me, bending and shifting with the movement of the streetlights. I told myself it was paranoia. Just the brain playing tricks, as it so often did.

I picked up my pace.

By the time I reached my apartment building, my heart was racing. I fumbled with the key, my fingers suddenly clumsy and uncooperative. The hallway was empty—of course it was—but the silence felt heavier than it had that morning. I locked the door behind me and bolted it for good measure, the metallic click echoing louder than it should have.

The fridge greeted me with its usual hum, indifferent as always. I set my bag down and collapsed into the chair by the window. My reflection in the glass was barely visible, a pale silhouette against the faint glow of the streetlights outside. I stared at it for a moment, trying to decide if it looked more like me or less.

The feeling of being watched lingered, clinging to the corners of my mind like cobwebs I couldn't quite sweep away. I told myself it was nothing, just nerves from the first day. Tomorrow would be better. It had to be.

I turned off the light and sat in the dark, listening to the hum of the fridge, the faint creak of the building settling, and my own uneven breathing. Somewhere outside, a car alarm blared briefly, then stopped. I waited for something else to happen, but nothing did.

Eventually, I went to bed, though sleep didn't come easily. I lay there, staring at the ceiling, counting the seconds until morning.

One. Two. Three. Four.

Chapter 3: Unspoken Resentments

Family dinners were like attending a play where everyone knew their role except me. My sisters would glide through the conversations effortlessly, reciting their lines with the kind of confidence that made it impossible to tell if they'd been rehearsing or were just naturally gifted at being perfect. My parents, the audience and occasional co-directors, would nod approvingly at every achievement, every anecdote, every life update. I, on the other hand, sat at the table like an understudy who hadn't even been given the script.

The smell of roast chicken filled the dining room as my mother bustled between the kitchen and the table. She carried a bowl of peas in one hand and a triumphant smile in the other. "Dinner's ready!" she chirped, as though we couldn't already see the food laid out before us.

My younger sisters, Emily and Sarah, were already seated, their plates perfectly portioned with an Instagram-worthy balance of protein, carbs, and greens. Emily was talking about a promotion she'd just received at work, her voice light and full of just the right amount of modesty. Sarah chimed in with a story about her upcoming trip abroad, seamlessly steering the conversation toward her volunteer work with underprivileged communities.

"And what about you?" my mother asked, turning to me with the kind of smile that could double as a stage light.

What about me? I wanted to say. What exactly did they want to hear? That I'd spent the week counting tiles in my bathroom? That I was on a first-name basis with the stains on my carpet? I picked up my fork and poked at the peas on my plate, pretending I hadn't heard the question.

"Work's fine," I said finally, offering as little detail as possible. It wasn't a lie. Work was fine. Fine in the same way a lukewarm cup of coffee is fine—technically acceptable but not particularly enjoyable.

My mother nodded, clearly unsatisfied but unwilling to press further. The spotlight shifted back to Emily, who was now recounting a story about her boss and the time she single-handedly saved an important project. I tuned out, focusing instead on the peas in front of me. There were seventeen of them. A number that felt simultaneously too small and too large for such an insignificant vegetable.

I started rearranging them into groups of four, trying to create a pattern that made sense. Four, four, four, and then...five. Damn it. The odd one out stared back at me like it knew I was struggling. I debated whether to eat it just to restore balance, but that would mean actually engaging with the food, which seemed like too much effort.

The conversation swirled around me, a blur of words and laughter that I couldn't quite grasp. Emily and Sarah's voices wove together like a well-rehearsed duet, their stories overlapping in a way that felt natural rather than competitive. They talked about their plans, their achievements, their lives, and I couldn't help but feel like a ghost at the table, present but invisible.

I caught snippets here and there—Sarah's plans to hike a mountain I couldn't pronounce, Emily's story about a client who "just loved her energy." My father nodded along, his expression one of quiet pride. My mother chimed in occasionally, adding just the right amount of encouragement to keep the momentum going.

No one asked me a follow-up question about work. I wasn't sure if I was relieved or insulted.

By the time dessert arrived—apple pie, of course—I had mentally checked out completely. The peas were still sitting in their uneven groups on my plate, a monument to my failure to create order from chaos. I shifted them around absentmindedly, trying to make the groups even again, but my heart wasn't in it.

As I reached for a slice of pie, my mother's voice cut through the din. "Are you sleeping enough?" she asked, her tone light but pointed.

The question caught me off guard. It felt too personal, too direct, like she'd somehow seen through the carefully constructed wall of indifference I'd built around myself. I hesitated, my hand hovering over the pie server.

"I'm fine," I said, a little too quickly.

Her eyes lingered on me for a moment longer than I was comfortable with before she nodded and turned her attention back to the table. The moment passed, but the sting of the question lingered, like a splinter I couldn't quite dislodge.

I left shortly after dessert, mumbling something about an early morning and ignoring the polite protests from my parents. Emily and Sarah waved goodbye with the kind of effortless grace I could never quite muster, their smiles genuine but not particularly invested. My mother gave me a quick hug at the door, her hands briefly gripping my shoulders as though she wanted to say something else but decided against it.

The walk back to my apartment was quiet, the kind of quiet that felt heavier than it should. The city was alive around me—cars honking, people talking, lights flickering—but it all felt distant, like I was walking through a poorly rendered simulation of reality.

I replayed my mother's question in my head, trying to figure out why it bothered me so much. Maybe it was the implication that she'd noticed something was wrong. Or maybe it was the realization that she cared enough to ask but not enough to press further. Either way, it stuck with me, an unwelcome echo that followed me all the way home.

By the time I reached my apartment, I was too tired to do anything but collapse into the chair by the window. The fridge hummed its usual greeting, indifferent as ever. I stared out at the street below, watching the headlights of passing cars stretch and blur like streaks of light in a time-lapse photo.

I thought about the peas, the uneven groups, the way they refused to align no matter how hard I tried. I thought about my sisters, their perfectly balanced lives, their ability to make everything look so effortless. And I thought about my mother, her question hanging in the air like a thread waiting to be pulled.

"Are you sleeping enough?"

I didn't have an answer. Not one that mattered, anyway.

The room felt too quiet again. The weight on my chest was back, heavier than before. I counted my breaths, hoping to calm myself. One. Two. Three.

I stared at the ceiling until the cracks blurred together, letting the fridge's hum drown out the noise in my head. The world outside carried on, oblivious, while I sat in the dark and tried to convince myself that everything was fine.

It wasn't. But at least no one expected me to say so.

Chapter 4: The Apartment Rituals Begin

The apartment was mine, but it didn't feel like mine. It felt like a space I was borrowing, one I wasn't entirely sure I was allowed to occupy. I couldn't change the beige walls, the wobbly table, or the smell of onions that had somehow seeped into the very foundation of the place. But I could rearrange the small, insignificant things to make it feel less alien, less temporary.

Order. That's what the apartment needed—an arrangement that made sense, a system that would give everything a place and, by extension, give me a place. So, I got to work.

The first step was the bookshelf. Alphabetical wasn't enough; it felt too rigid, like a librarian's daydream. Instead, I sorted the books by genre, then by size, then by the likelihood of me actually reading them again. When I was done, the shelf looked like a miniature city skyline, with paperbacks forming tidy suburbs around the towering hardcovers.

Next came the kitchen drawers. The utensils went into their designated slots: forks with forks, knives with knives. But the spoons were tricky—big spoons and small spoons, teaspoons and soup spoons. I wasn't sure if soup spoons deserved their own category, but I decided to risk it. The drawer slid closed with a satisfying thunk, and for the first time in days, I felt like I'd accomplished something.

The living room came next. By "living room," I mean the corner of the apartment where the chair and wobbly table lived. I centered the table on the rug, adjusted the chair to face the window, and spent an embarrassing amount of time making sure the angles were perfect. It wasn't much, but it was symmetrical, and that was enough.

By the time I reached the desk in my bedroom, the sun had dipped below the horizon, casting the room in a faint, bluish light. The desk was the last piece of the puzzle, the place where I'd theoretically get work done—if I ever found work worth doing. It was also where I'd dumped all the things I hadn't bothered unpacking yet: pens, loose papers, a random collection of odds and ends that didn't belong anywhere else.

I started with the pens, testing each one to see if it still worked. The dead ones went into the trash, while the survivors were sorted into categories: black ink, blue ink, and miscellaneous. A small notebook joined the pens in the "practical" pile, while a half-used roll of tape and a stray button migrated to the "what do I do with this?" pile.

As I worked, I felt a strange sense of calm settle over me. The rhythm of sorting, organizing, and arranging was soothing in a way I couldn't quite explain. It was like putting together a jigsaw puzzle, except the pieces were my life, and the image was whatever I wanted it to be.

It was when I went to throw away a handful of crumpled papers that I noticed it: a small tear on the cuff of my shirt.

At first, it didn't register. It was just a faint line of frayed fabric, no bigger than the edge of a thumbnail. But the more I stared at it, the more it gnawed at me. I didn't remember tearing it. I didn't remember anything that could have caused it.

I ran my thumb along the edge of the tear, feeling the roughness of the threads. It wasn't an old tear; it was new, fresh. But from what? I replayed the day in my head, searching for anything that might explain it. Had I caught it on a nail? A sharp edge? But there was nothing. Just the tear, sitting there like a question I couldn't answer.

I shook my head and tossed the papers into the trash, telling myself it didn't matter. It was just a shirt. A shirt I barely liked, anyway. But as I returned to the desk, the tear lingered in the back of my mind, a small splinter of unease that refused to dislodge.

By the time I finished organizing the desk, it was almost midnight. The pens were lined up in perfect rows, the papers neatly stacked, and the odd items tucked away in a drawer labeled "Miscellaneous." The desk looked immaculate, a tiny island of order in a sea of uncertainty.

I stood back and admired my work, feeling a flicker of satisfaction. This was it. This was how I'd make the apartment mine. Not through big changes or bold declarations, but through small, precise acts of control. If I could organize the desk, the bookshelf, the kitchen drawers—then maybe, just maybe, I could organize myself.

I sat down in the chair and rested my hands on the surface of the desk. The room was quiet, save for the faint hum of the fridge in the kitchen. I closed my eyes and let the silence wash over me, trying to ignore the nagging feeling that something was still out of place.

I woke up an hour later, slumped over the desk with a crick in my neck and a faint ache in my back. The tear in the shirt greeted me like an unwelcome guest, its edges slightly more frayed than before. I rubbed my eyes and stood up, stretching the stiffness from my limbs.

The apartment was dark, the kind of dark that made the shadows feel heavier than they should. I glanced at the window, half-expecting to see something—or someone—standing there, but the street below was empty. Just the usual glow of streetlights and the faint rustle of wind through the alley.

I shook my head and made my way to bed, the tear still tugging at the edges of my thoughts. It was nothing, I told myself. Just a loose thread, a coincidence, a meaningless detail. But as I lay staring at the cracks in the ceiling, I couldn't shake the feeling that the apartment was watching me, waiting for me to notice something I hadn't yet seen.

The next morning, the tear was still there. The desk was still perfect. The apartment was still mine. But none of it felt quite right.

Chapter 5: The First Slip

The first bill slipped through my fingers like a single raindrop that precedes a storm. It wasn't intentional—I wasn't the type to ignore things like that. Bills, like clockwork, had their rightful place in the fragile ecosystem of my life. But somehow, this one crept past me.

The notification came via email, the subject line shouting in all caps: PAST DUE: URGENT ACTION REQUIRED. It felt like being caught in a lie I didn't know I'd told. The amount wasn't enormous—nothing that would bankrupt me on the spot—but it was enough to throw off the delicate, imaginary budget I'd constructed in my head.

I sat at the desk, the email open on my laptop, staring at the number like it might rearrange itself into something less terrifying if I gave it enough time. It didn't. It just sat there, glaring at me, a debt I hadn't accounted for.

"Okay," I muttered aloud, because sometimes speaking to no one made me feel like I had company. "This is fine. It's just math."

Math was, theoretically, manageable. Numbers had rules. They were logical, predictable. You added, subtracted, and eventually arrived at a solution. But this solution felt slippery, just out of reach. Every attempt to balance the scales left me feeling further behind.

I grabbed my notebook and started jotting down figures, scribbling furiously as if speed alone could fix the problem. Income. Expenses. Debts. Potential savings. I wrote them all out, line after line, until the page blurred with equations and symbols. Somewhere along the way, the calculations stopped making sense.

By the time I looked up, hours had passed. The notebook sat in front of me, filled with numbers that no longer seemed real. The amount I owed had multiplied in my mind, ballooning into something monstrous. I flipped to a fresh page and started again, convinced I'd made a mistake. There had to be an error, a decimal point in the wrong place, something I could fix.

But there wasn't. The numbers didn't lie. They didn't care.

The pacing started after the third attempt at recalculating. I stood up, stretched my legs, and began moving in slow circles around the apartment. One, two, three steps to the window. Four, five, six steps to the fridge. Seven, eight, nine back to the desk. I counted them aloud, a low murmur that echoed in the otherwise silent room. The repetition was soothing, like a chant, though it did little to quiet the storm in my head.

Somewhere around lap thirty, I paused mid-step, a flicker of something sharp cutting through my thoughts. It wasn't a memory exactly, more like the ghost of one—a flash of darkness, an alley illuminated by the pale glow of a single streetlight. I could hear footsteps, faint but deliberate, echoing against brick walls.

I shook my head and kept walking. It was nothing. Just a stray thought, the byproduct of an overworked mind. But it came again, clearer this time: the alley, the footsteps, the sound of something wet hitting the pavement. My chest tightened as I tried to place the memory, to pin it down. It slipped away, leaving only the faint impression of unease in its wake.

I returned to the desk, determined to finish what I'd started. The numbers stared back at me, as unforgiving as ever. I tapped the pen against the edge of the notebook, the rhythmic click-click-click filling the silence. My eyes drifted to the corner of the desk, where the knife sat. I hadn't put it there—it had been sitting there since I'd found it a few nights ago, gleaming softly in the dim light.

Its presence felt oddly reassuring, though I couldn't explain why. It was just a knife, a tool, something sharp and utilitarian. But tonight, it seemed heavier, more significant. I reached out and picked it up, turning it over in my hands. The weight was familiar now, almost comforting. I ran my thumb along the edge, feeling the sharpness bite into my skin without breaking it.

The sound of footsteps returned, faint but insistent, like an echo bouncing through the recesses of my mind. I froze, the knife still in my hand, and listened. Nothing. Just the hum of the fridge and the distant murmur of traffic outside.

I set the knife back on the desk and stood up again, my legs restless. The pacing resumed, though the rhythm felt uneven now. One, two, three steps to the window. Four, five, six to the fridge. Seven, eight—pause. I turned toward the door, half-expecting to see someone standing there, though I knew it was ridiculous. The hallway outside was empty. It had to be.

By the time I finally sat down again, my chest ached from the tension I hadn't realized I was holding. The notebook was still open, the numbers taunting me with their unchangeable certainty. I stared at them for what felt like an eternity, willing them to rearrange themselves into something manageable. They didn't.

The email notification blinked on the laptop screen, a reminder I couldn't ignore. The past-due bill, the looming debt, the inescapable weight of it all. I clicked the email closed, shoved the notebook into a drawer, and turned off the desk lamp. The darkness felt heavier than usual, pressing against my shoulders like a physical force.

I climbed into bed and stared at the ceiling, counting the cracks to calm myself. One, two, three. The pacing footsteps in my head followed me, fading in and out like the rhythm of a distant heartbeat. I squeezed my eyes shut and tried to push the image of the alley away, but it clung to the edges of my mind, refusing to let go.

The night stretched on, long and unforgiving. When sleep finally came, it was filled with shadows and the echo of footsteps, always just out of reach.

Chapter 6: The Burden of Masking

Work was a performance, and I was a decent actor. Not great—no standing ovations or awards ceremonies—but I knew how to hit my marks, deliver my lines, and blend into the ensemble. If someone were watching closely, they might notice the cracks in my performance: the occasional hesitation, the forced smile, the way I mimicked others just a beat too late. But no one was watching. They were all too busy starring in their own shows.

Mirroring was my specialty. When Susan, my manager, laughed at something, I made sure to laugh too, matching her tone and volume as best I could. When a coworker leaned on their desk during small talk, I leaned on mine. It wasn't deception exactly, more like adaptation—a way to make sure I didn't stick out.

The effort was exhausting.

By noon, I was already worn down, my brain a sluggish machine trying to keep up with the constant calculations. Every interaction felt like solving a complex equation, except the variables were people, and the solution was survival.

Take lunch, for example. The breakroom was a minefield of potential missteps. Do you sit alone and risk looking unfriendly? Or do you sit with someone and risk saying something awkward? I usually chose the former, parking myself in the corner with my sandwich and a book I wasn't actually reading. Today, however, one of my coworkers, Karen, sat at the table next to me.

"How's it going?" she asked, her voice bright and chirpy, like a bird that had accidentally wandered into a cubicle farm.

"Good," I said, mimicking her tone. I took a bite of my sandwich to avoid elaborating.

She nodded and started talking about her weekend plans, something involving her dog and a new park she'd discovered. I nodded along, throwing in the occasional "Oh, nice" or "Sounds fun" to keep the conversation alive without actually contributing.

When she laughed at her own story, I laughed too, though it felt hollow coming out of my mouth. My laugh wasn't for her—it was for me. A way to blend in, to reassure her that I was normal, that I wasn't silently cataloging the number of times she said the word "adorable" (four, for the record).

By the time the workday ended, I was a drained battery. The act of mirroring, adjusting, pretending—it took everything I had, and then some. My body moved on autopilot as I gathered my things and left the office, stepping into the cool evening air like a swimmer breaking the surface after holding their breath too long.

The city was alive with its usual buzz of noise and motion. Cars honked, people chattered, the occasional siren wailed in the distance. I walked quickly, counting my steps as I went: one, two, three, four. The rhythm was soothing, a steady beat to drown out the static in my head.

I passed a newsstand on the corner, its display lit by the harsh glow of a fluorescent bulb. The headline caught my eye: "UNSOLVED MURDER BAFFLES POLICE" in bold, blocky letters. Below it was a grainy photo of a dimly lit alley, the kind you'd find in a noir film or a nightmare.

My pace slowed, and for a moment, I couldn't look away. The image felt familiar, though I couldn't place why. The alley, the shadows, the faint glow of a streetlight—it all tugged at something in the back of my mind, like a memory trying to surface but not quite making it.

I shook my head and walked faster.

The feeling of being watched crept up on me again, prickling the back of my neck like an unwanted hand. I glanced over my shoulder, half-expecting to see someone following me, but the sidewalk was empty. Just the usual mix of strangers hurrying home or lingering too long in places they didn't belong.

I turned the corner onto a quieter street, my steps quickening. The newsstand headline replayed itself in my head, the bold letters flashing like a warning sign: UNSOLVED MURDER. My thoughts shifted to the flashes I'd been seeing lately—the alley, the footsteps, the sound of something wet hitting the ground.

It wasn't real, I told myself. Just an overactive imagination. Stress. Sleep deprivation. Anything but what my brain was trying to suggest.

When I reached my apartment building, I felt like I'd just finished a marathon. My legs ached, my chest was tight, and my hands trembled slightly as I unlocked the door. Inside, the familiar hum of the fridge greeted me, a small but reliable constant in an otherwise unpredictable world.

I dropped my bag by the door and sat at the desk, staring at the knife. It was still there, exactly where I'd left it, its blade catching the dim light like it had something to say. I picked it up and turned it over in my hands, feeling the weight of it, the coldness of the metal against my skin.

For a moment, I thought about the newsstand headline again, the grainy photo of the alley, the fragments of memory that felt more real than they should. My grip on the knife tightened.

I set the knife down and leaned back in the chair, closing my eyes. The images danced in the darkness behind my eyelids: the alley, the footsteps, the shadows stretching long and thin under the flickering glow of a streetlight. I tried to push them away, but they clung to the edges of my mind, stubborn and unrelenting.

When I opened my eyes, the room felt too quiet. The hum of the fridge was still there, but it sounded distant, like it was coming from another room entirely. I glanced at the window, half-expecting to see a face staring back at me, but there was nothing. Just the faint outline of my own reflection, pale and distorted.

I turned off the light and went to bed, though I knew sleep wouldn't come easily. The weight of the day pressed down on me, heavy and suffocating, as I lay staring at the ceiling. The last thing I saw before I drifted off was the knife, its blade glinting faintly in the moonlight.

The last thing I heard was the echo of footsteps, growing fainter but never quite disappearing.

Chapter 7: The Stranger in the Hallway

The hallway was quiet, as it always was. The dim, flickering light above the elevator cast long, uneven shadows against the walls, giving the space an eerie, half-abandoned look. I stepped out of my apartment, locking the door behind me, and immediately felt it—the sensation that someone was watching.

It wasn't the vague paranoia I sometimes carried with me like a frayed jacket. This was sharper, heavier. My pulse quickened as I turned my head, and there he was.

A man stood at the far end of the hallway, half-hidden in shadow. He wasn't doing anything, just standing there with his hands shoved into his coat pockets, his face partially obscured by the brim of a hat. But the way he stood, so perfectly still, felt deliberate. Intentional. His eyes—or at least what I could see of them—were locked on me.

For a moment, neither of us moved. My fingers hovered over the lock, frozen mid-turn, as I tried to decide whether to ignore him or acknowledge him. A polite nod? A casual "hello"? Nothing seemed appropriate for a man who looked like he belonged in a black-and-white crime drama, waiting for a cue that would never come.

I finished locking the door, the metallic click louder than usual in the stillness. My hands trembled slightly as I shoved the key into my pocket, my every movement feeling exaggerated under his gaze. He hadn't moved an inch.

It wasn't unusual to see neighbors in the hallway. I'd passed plenty of them before—a nod, a quick "hi," and we'd go our separate ways. But this was different. This wasn't casual. The way he stared wasn't neighborly; it was like he was waiting for something. For me to speak, to act, to slip up.

I took a hesitant step forward, my sneakers squeaking against the polished floor. He didn't react. Just stood there, still as a statue, the brim of his hat casting a shadow across his face. I couldn't see his expression, but I didn't need to. His presence was enough.

The memory came suddenly, uninvited and incomplete: the sound of footsteps behind me on a dark street. Quick, deliberate, matching my own. The feeling of being followed, my pulse racing as I turned a corner, hoping to lose whoever—or whatever—was behind me. The memory faded as quickly as it had arrived, leaving behind a familiar unease.

I shook my head, trying to dismiss it. It wasn't real. Just my overactive imagination, piecing together fragments of anxiety and sleepless nights into something more sinister. The man in the hallway wasn't following me. He couldn't be. He was just...there.

Still, the sensation of being watched clung to me like static electricity, making my skin crawl. I glanced at him one last time before heading toward the elevator, my steps quick and deliberate. The elevator dinged, its doors sliding open with a mechanical groan, and I stepped inside without looking back.

The ride down was suffocatingly slow. The elevator creaked and groaned, its fluorescent light flickering above me. I stared at my reflection in the mirrored walls, my face pale and drawn.

I looked like someone who hadn't slept in days—which wasn't far from the truth.

As the doors slid open to the lobby, I couldn't shake the image of the man in the hallway. His stillness, his silence, the way he seemed to absorb the light around him. It was probably nothing, I told myself. Just a neighbor with nowhere to be. But the thought didn't stick. My mind kept circling back to the way he'd stared, the way his presence had felt less like coincidence and more like judgment.

The city was bustling outside, the noise and motion a contrast to the eerie stillness of the hallway. Cars honked, pedestrians weaved through the streets, and the air smelled faintly of gasoline and damp concrete. I welcomed the chaos—it felt alive, unpredictable, human.

But even in the noise, the man lingered in my mind. His shadow stretched across my thoughts, tall and unmoving. I told myself it didn't matter, that he was just some guy I'd never see again. But as I turned a corner and caught my reflection in a shop window, I couldn't help but notice the tension in my posture, the way my shoulders hunched as if bracing for something.

When I returned to the apartment later that evening, the hallway was empty. The flickering light above the elevator cast the same uneven shadows, but the space felt different. Lighter. Less oppressive.

Still, I hesitated at the door to my apartment, my key hovering over the lock. I glanced over my shoulder, half-expecting to see the man again, but there was nothing. Just the faint hum of the building's heating system and the muffled sound of a television from one of the other units.

I stepped inside and locked the door behind me, the deadbolt sliding into place with a satisfying click. My bag dropped to the floor, and I leaned against the door for a moment, letting out a breath I hadn't realized I'd been holding.

The fridge hummed softly in the kitchen, a constant presence in the background of my life. I sat at the desk, the knife still resting where I'd left it. Its blade caught the light, gleaming faintly, almost beckoning. I picked it up, turning it over in my hands, the weight familiar now. Comforting.

The memory of the footsteps returned, stronger this time. The dark alley, the quickened pace, the sound of my breathing loud in my ears. I couldn't tell if it was real or something my mind had conjured, a phantom stitched together from scraps of fear and imagination.

The knife felt heavier than usual as I set it back on the desk. I stared at it for a long time, the hum of the fridge filling the silence.

Sleep didn't come easily that night. I lay in bed, staring at the ceiling, the cracks forming shapes I couldn't quite name. The image of the man in the hallway replayed in my mind, his stillness, his stare, the way he'd seemed to see through me.

When I finally drifted off, it was with the faint echo of footsteps in my ears, growing louder as they followed me into the dark.

Chapter 8: A Growing Distance

F amily invitations used to come with alarming frequency, filling my phone with notifications that I dutifully ignored until guilt forced me to reply. "Can't make it this time," I'd write, always with a vague excuse about work or being busy, even when my calendar was as empty as my fridge. At first, they'd try to prod—"Next time for sure?"—but eventually, the messages became less insistent, the invitations less frequent. Now, weeks passed without a single one.

It wasn't as though I didn't love my family—or at least the idea of them. But the thought of sitting through another dinner, navigating their questions and their smiles and their carefully curated stories, felt like trying to breathe through a straw. I could already hear my mother's soft sighs when I avoided her gaze, my sisters' laughter that always seemed a little too bright, a little too perfect.

So when my phone buzzed with a new message from Emily, I didn't even bother opening it. The notification stared back at me for a moment, a silent accusation, before I swiped it away. It joined the others in the digital purgatory of unread texts and voicemails, a growing pile of evidence that I was failing at something I couldn't quite name.

That evening, the apartment felt heavier than usual, the silence pressing against me like an unwelcome guest. I tried distracting myself with the usual rituals: rearranging the bookshelves, counting the tiles in the bathroom, aligning the pens on my desk. But even the familiar rhythms couldn't shake the nagging sense of something missing.

The knife sat on the desk, its presence growing more intrusive with each passing day. I hadn't moved it since I first placed it there, yet it seemed to occupy more space than it should, its gleaming blade catching the dim light like a quiet reminder of something I didn't want to remember.

I went to bed early, though I knew sleep wouldn't come easily. The sheets felt too rough, the pillow too flat, the cracks in the ceiling forming shapes I couldn't unsee. I closed my eyes and tried to focus on my breathing—one, two, three—but the rhythm faltered, replaced by the steady drip of something wet.

In the dream, my hands were slick with blood. It dripped from my fingertips, pooling on the floor in dark, shimmering puddles. I couldn't see where it came from or why it was there, but the sight of it filled me with a strange mix of fear and resignation.

There were flashes—brief, disjointed images that didn't make sense. The glint of a blade. The sound of footsteps echoing in an alley. A muffled cry, sharp and fleeting. I tried to piece them together, but they slipped through my fingers like water, leaving only the blood behind.

I stared at my hands, watching the droplets fall in slow motion, each one landing with a sound that was too loud, too real. The scene felt familiar, though I couldn't say why. It was like replaying a memory I didn't remember making, a ghost of something that might not have happened.

I woke up with a start, my chest tight and my pulse racing. The room was dark, the faint hum of the fridge the only sound. I sat up and looked at my hands, half-expecting to see them stained red. They weren't. Just the usual pale skin, trembling slightly as I ran them through my hair.

The dream lingered, clinging to the edges of my mind like a shadow I couldn't shake. It didn't feel like a dream, not entirely. There was a weight to it, a sense of something unfinished, like a story I'd walked into halfway through.

I glanced at the desk, at the knife that sat there so innocently, its blade reflecting the faint glow of the streetlights outside. It hadn't moved, of course, but it felt closer somehow, as though it had crept forward while I wasn't looking.

The phone buzzed on the nightstand, the screen lighting up with another message from Emily. I didn't read it. Instead, I turned the phone face down and stared at the ceiling, counting the cracks until the dream blurred into the haze of exhaustion.

Somewhere in the distance, I thought I heard the echo of footsteps. Faint, deliberate, growing louder before fading into silence.

Chapter 9: Numbers as Refuge

Numbers were safe. Numbers made sense. They didn't judge, they didn't lie, and they didn't change based on mood or whim. If the rest of my life felt like a chaotic storm, numbers were the eye—the calm center I could retreat to when everything else became too loud.

I started small, as I always did. Counting steps to the kitchen in the morning: ten, unless I veered slightly to avoid the corner of the rug, in which case it became eleven. The tiles in the bathroom remained steadfast at eighteen. My walk to work was 437 steps, though that depended on whether I stopped to wait for the traffic light or jaywalked when no one was looking.

It wasn't just counting, though. Numbers became their own language, a way to assign meaning to things that otherwise felt meaningless. Five was stability—solid, grounded, unshakable. Seven was balance, the midpoint between too much and not enough. Nine was chaos, the tipping point where order unraveled.

My desk at work became a carefully curated sanctuary. Pens lined up in groups of three (practical, efficient), papers stacked in fours (predictable, reliable). Even my coffee breaks had their own rhythm—eight minutes precisely, no more, no less. I didn't think of it as obsessive. It was just...necessary. A way to maintain control when control felt like a fleeting luxury.

But the flashes started anyway.

They came without warning, like sudden gusts of wind that knocked the breath out of me. I'd be midway through a calculation—adding the hours I'd worked this week or subtracting my expenses from my paycheck—and suddenly, the numbers would fade, replaced by indistinct faces.

Blurred and panicked, they hovered just out of reach, their expressions twisting into something I couldn't quite read. Sometimes they were screaming, though the sound was muffled, like hearing someone shout underwater. Other times, they were silent, their mouths moving but no words coming out.

I'd blink, shake my head, try to push them away. But they lingered, clinging to the edges of my vision like static.

One afternoon at work, while sorting through a stack of invoices, it happened again. I was halfway through calculating the total—$2,349.76—when the numbers dissolved into nothingness, replaced by a face. It was a woman this time, her features smeared and indistinct, her eyes wide with fear. She reached out, her hand blurred like a glitch in a video, before disappearing entirely.

"Everything okay?" Karen's voice snapped me back to reality.

I looked up, blinking rapidly, my heart pounding in my chest. Karen stood by the doorway, a cup of coffee in her hand, her expression curious but not concerned.

"Yeah," I said, forcing a smile that felt like it might crack my face. "Just...zoned out for a second."

She nodded and walked away, leaving me alone with the stack of invoices and the ghost of a face that no longer existed.

At home, the numbers felt more fragile, less reliable. I tried to count the steps to the fridge—ten, eleven, twelve—but the rhythm faltered when I saw a shadow in the corner of my eye.

I turned quickly, but there was nothing there. Just the empty apartment, its walls beige and indifferent.

I sat at the desk, the knife glinting faintly under the dim light. I hadn't moved it, but it felt more present now, its blade catching my eye like it was waiting for something. I picked it up, running my thumb along the edge, feeling the sharpness bite into my skin without breaking it.

The faces came again, more vivid this time. A man, his mouth open in a silent scream. A woman, her hand clutching at her throat. A blur of motion, the glint of metal, the sound of something wet hitting the ground.

I dropped the knife and stood up abruptly, my chair scraping against the floor. My breaths came fast and shallow as I paced the apartment, counting my steps in a desperate attempt to anchor myself. One, two, three, four. Five, six, seven. The rhythm steadied me, pulling me back from the edge.

The fridge hummed softly in the background as I returned to the desk. I picked up the knife again, turning it over in my hands, the weight of it strangely comforting. The numbers still danced in my mind, a mix of equations and fragments of something I couldn't name.

$2,349.76.

437 steps.

One. Two. Three.

The knife's blade gleamed under the light, its edge sharp and unforgiving. I set it down carefully, aligning it perfectly with the edge of the desk.

Numbers were safe. Numbers made sense.

But the faces...they didn't.

That night, as I lay in bed, the flashes returned. The faces, the alley, the knife. They blended together into a dreamscape that felt more real than the world I woke up to.

When I opened my eyes, the ceiling cracks stared back at me, their jagged lines forming patterns I couldn't unsee. I counted them, trying to drown out the images with numbers.

One. Two. Three.

But the faces lingered, haunting the edges of my mind.

Chapter 10: The Weight of Debt

The bills started arriving in clusters, like a swarm of flies circling something rotten. Each envelope bore the same ominous greeting: Past Due. Final Notice. Immediate Action Required. The bold letters felt like they were yelling at me, demanding a level of attention I wasn't ready to give.

I lined them up on the desk, arranging them by size and severity, their stark white envelopes contrasting sharply with the dark wood. Rent. Utilities. Credit card minimum payments. They stared back at me like an accusation, silent but damning.

The total amount was staggering. I'd known it was bad, of course—I'd felt it in the way my account balance seemed to evaporate faster month after month, the way I avoided looking at my bank app like it might bite me. But seeing the numbers all together, neatly written in black ink, was something else entirely.

$14,872.59.

I wrote the number at the top of my notebook, circling it with a shaky hand. It was an impossible number, a mountain I had no hope of climbing. I tried breaking it down into smaller pieces—divide and conquer, as they say—but even the fragments were overwhelming. Rent alone took up nearly half of my income, and the rest was devoured by interest rates and late fees.

I flipped to a new page and started recalculating, convinced I'd made a mistake. Maybe I'd double-counted something, or maybe there was a hidden error waiting to be uncovered. But no matter how many times I added, subtracted, and divided, the number refused to budge.

$14,872.59.

The pacing started again, a familiar rhythm that carried me from the desk to the fridge and back. One, two, three, four steps. Five, six, seven, eight. The numbers helped, their steady beat keeping the panic at bay. But tonight, even they felt fragile, like they might shatter under the weight of what I owed.

As I passed the window, a flicker of motion caught my eye. For a split second, I thought I saw someone standing in the alley below, their silhouette barely visible in the dim light. I stopped mid-step, my breath catching in my throat, but when I looked again, the alley was empty.

I shook my head and kept walking.

Back at the desk, the knife sat in its usual spot, its blade catching the faint glow of the desk lamp. I picked it up, turning it over in my hands, the weight of it grounding me. The feel of the cold metal against my skin was strangely reassuring, a reminder that some things were solid, tangible, unchanging.

That's when the memories surfaced.

They came in fragments, disjointed and fleeting, like pieces of a puzzle that didn't quite fit together. A dark street, the faint glow of a streetlight, the metallic tang of blood in the air. My hands, slick and trembling, clutching something I couldn't identify.

I closed my eyes, trying to push the images away. They weren't real. They couldn't be. Just the product of an overactive imagination, fueled by stress and lack of sleep.

When I opened my eyes, the knife was still in my hand, its blade glinting like it knew something I didn't. I set it down carefully, aligning it with the edge of the desk, and returned my focus to the notebook.

$14,872.59.

I underlined the number twice, as if that might make it easier to deal with. It didn't.

The night stretched on, long and oppressive. I tried recalculating again, then again, each attempt more frantic than the last. The numbers blurred together, the ink smudging under my fingers as I scribbled and erased, scribbled and erased. Somewhere in the chaos, I lost track of the time.

The fridge hummed softly in the background, a constant reminder of the world outside my mind. I glanced at it briefly, half-expecting it to have an answer for me, but it offered nothing.

My thoughts drifted back to the dark street, the faint metallic tang, the blurred outlines of faces I couldn't quite make out. They felt too real to be imagined, too vivid to dismiss entirely. But if they were real, then what did that mean?

I shook my head, forcing myself to focus on the page in front of me. Numbers were safe. Numbers made sense. I could control them, even if I couldn't control anything else.

By the time I finally put the notebook down, my hands were trembling. The number still stared back at me, unyielding and unforgiving. $14,872.59. It didn't care about my calculations or my pacing or the fragments of memory clawing at the edges of my mind.

I turned off the desk lamp and sat in the dark, the knife's silhouette barely visible against the wood. The weight of the debt pressed down on me, heavy and suffocating, as I closed my eyes and tried to focus on my breathing.

One, two, three, four.

In the silence, I thought I heard footsteps again, faint and distant, echoing through the recesses of my mind.

Chapter 11: A Failed Connection

I wasn't sure why I'd agreed to the date in the first place. Maybe it was the nagging voice in the back of my head telling me I needed to try, to make some kind of effort to connect with the world outside my apartment. Or maybe I just wanted to prove to myself that I wasn't as isolated as I felt.

We met at a small café, the kind of place with mismatched furniture and overpriced lattes that made you feel cultured just for being there. His name was Nathan. He had kind eyes, a warm laugh, and an easy way of filling silences that would have been awkward with anyone else. In theory, it should have worked.

But theory and reality rarely got along.

"I feel like I've been talking this whole time," Nathan said, smiling as he sipped his coffee. "Tell me about you."

I froze, my mind scrambling for something to say. What was there to tell? My life wasn't exactly brimming with interesting anecdotes. I couldn't very well say, Well, I spend most of my time counting tiles in my bathroom and convincing myself the knife on my desk isn't whispering to me.

"Not much to tell," I said finally, offering a weak smile. "I work a lot."

"Where do you work?"

"A...a desk job." Technically true, though it felt like a lie in the way it omitted so much. "It's not very exciting."

Nathan tilted his head, studying me with a curious expression. "What do you like to do when you're not working?"

I could feel the mask slipping, the carefully constructed facade cracking under the weight of his gaze. "You know, just...normal stuff. Reading. Watching TV." I hesitated, then added, "Counting things."

"Counting things?" he echoed, his smile faltering slightly.

"Steps, mostly. Or tiles. It's just...a habit." The words felt clumsy and exposed, like a wound I hadn't meant to show. I quickly took a sip of my coffee, hoping to change the subject.

The rest of the date passed in a blur of half-hearted conversation and forced laughter. I tried to mirror his expressions, to match his tone, but it felt like trying to swim against a current that only grew stronger the harder I tried. By the time the check came, the energy between us had shifted into something strained and uncomfortable.

As we stood outside the café, Nathan hesitated, his hands tucked into the pockets of his jacket. "You're nice," he said finally. "But...I don't know. You seem kind of...distant."

The word hit harder than it should have. I forced a smile, nodding as though I agreed. "Yeah. I get that a lot."

He offered a polite goodbye, and I watched him walk away, disappearing into the sea of pedestrians on the sidewalk. For a moment, I stood there, rooted to the spot, wondering if I should have said something—anything—to change the outcome. But the truth was, he wasn't wrong. I was distant. And I didn't know how to be anything else.

The walk home was quieter than usual. The city's usual symphony of honking cars and chattering voices seemed muted, like someone had turned the volume down on the world. I counted my steps out of habit, the numbers steady and reassuring: one, two, three, four.

Halfway home, I noticed the footsteps.

At first, I thought they were mine, their rhythm syncing perfectly with my own. But then I stopped to tie my shoe, and the sound continued, faint but deliberate, echoing against the buildings around me. I straightened slowly, my heart pounding as I glanced over my shoulder.

The street was empty.

I shook my head and kept walking, telling myself it was nothing. Just a trick of the acoustics, or maybe someone turning a corner before I noticed. But the footsteps came again, closer this time. My breath quickened as I clutched my keys in my pocket, arranging them between my fingers like a makeshift weapon.

I turned sharply, my eyes scanning the street for any sign of movement. Shadows stretched long and thin under the streetlights, but there was no one there. Just me and the faint rustle of leaves in the breeze.

By the time I reached my apartment building, my chest was tight with a mix of panic and exhaustion. The hallway was as empty as the street had been, but the silence felt heavier here, pressing against me like a physical weight. I fumbled with my keys, my hands trembling as I unlocked the door and stepped inside.

The fridge hummed softly in the background, its usual indifference oddly comforting. I dropped my bag on the floor and sat at the desk, my head in my hands. The knife was still there, its blade catching the light like it was waiting for me to pick it up. I resisted the urge, instead staring at it like it might hold some kind of answer.

The footsteps lingered in my mind, their rhythm merging with the memory of Nathan's voice: You seem kind of...distant.

Maybe I was distant. Maybe that's what I needed to be.

That night, I dreamed of footsteps again, louder and closer than before. When I woke, the knife was still on the desk, its edge gleaming in the pale morning light.

And the world outside was just as quiet as I'd left it.

Chapter 12: The First Note

The days were starting to blend together, each one bleeding into the next like watercolors left out in the rain. Work. Home. Numbers. Walks. Steps. Bills. The rhythm of my life had become mechanical, a loop that repeated itself without deviation. Even the fridge's hum seemed synced to the monotony, a dull, persistent reminder of how little had changed.

I needed a way to break the cycle—or at least feel like I had. That's when the idea for the note came to me.

It wasn't profound, not by any stretch of the imagination. I grabbed a scrap of paper from the desk and scribbled three simple tasks:

Get up.

Go to work.

Pay the bill.

Each word felt like a command, sharp and unforgiving, but it also gave me a sense of purpose, however small. Tasks were manageable. Tasks could be completed, crossed off, erased. They didn't require emotional investment, just action.

I pinned the note to the fridge with a magnet shaped like a strawberry, its cheery design a stark contrast to the starkness of the words. For a moment, I stepped back and admired my work. There it was, staring back at me—a plan. A direction. Something tangible in a world that had felt increasingly intangible.

It offered relief, but only for a moment.

As I stood there, the weight of the knife in the drawer crept back into my mind. I hadn't touched it since that night—hadn't even opened the drawer. But its presence felt heavier than ever, like it was pressing against the thin layer of separation between us. I couldn't stop thinking about it, even as I tried to focus on the note.

Without fully deciding to, I found myself opening the drawer. The knife lay there, pristine and polished, its blade gleaming faintly under the dim light of the kitchen. It looked sharper than I remembered, cleaner, as if it had been scrubbed free of something I couldn't name.

I picked it up, turning it over in my hands. The weight was familiar now, almost comforting, though the comfort was laced with unease. The blade's edge caught the light, a thin line of silver that seemed to shimmer with intent.

Had I cleaned it? I didn't think so. I couldn't remember cleaning it. But the knife didn't look like it had been sitting in a drawer for weeks. It looked...fresh.

I set it back down carefully, the sound of the blade against the wood sending a faint shiver down my spine. The drawer closed with a soft thud, but the unease lingered, clinging to me like a shadow I couldn't shake. I turned back to the fridge, to the note, hoping its simplicity would ground me again.

"Get up. Go to work. Pay the bill."

The words stared back at me, steady and unchanging, a stark reminder of what needed to be done. But the relief I'd felt earlier was gone, replaced by the nagging sensation that something wasn't right. The note was supposed to help, to organize my thoughts, to give me a sense of control. Instead, it felt like a taunt, a challenge I wasn't sure I could meet.

I went to bed early that night, the note still pinned to the fridge, the knife still in its drawer. Sleep didn't come easily. I lay in the dark, staring at the cracks in the ceiling, my thoughts spiraling into shapes I couldn't name. The note, the knife, the bills—they all blurred together, merging into a single, oppressive weight that pressed down on my chest.

When I finally drifted off, my dreams were fragmented and chaotic. Shadows stretched long and thin, the sound of footsteps echoing in the distance. The knife glinted in the dark, its blade sharper than I remembered.

When I woke, the note was still on the fridge, the knife still in the drawer. Nothing had changed. But nothing felt the same.

Chapter 13: The Knife in the Drawer

Cleaning was supposed to be mindless, a way to occupy my hands and distract my thoughts. The apartment had begun to feel like it was suffocating me, the walls pressing closer with each passing day. Dust had settled into corners, and crumbs had gathered in the spaces between cushions. It felt like my mind had spilled out into my living space, leaving chaos in its wake.

I started in the kitchen, scrubbing the counters with a ferocity that bordered on obsessive. The fridge hummed softly, its usual indifference mocking my attempt at control. From there, I moved to the living room, vacuuming the rug and rearranging the furniture in patterns that felt more symmetrical. It was only when I reached the desk that I noticed the drawer.

I hesitated for a moment before pulling it open.

The knife lay inside, exactly where I'd left it—or at least, where I thought I'd left it. Its polished blade caught the light, gleaming as though it had been waiting for me. Something about it felt off, though I couldn't quite pinpoint why. The handle was smooth, unmarked, its black surface free of any scratches or fingerprints. The blade itself was pristine, almost unnaturally so, as if it had been cleaned recently.

But I hadn't touched it. Not since that night.

I picked it up, the weight of it familiar now, almost comforting. The cool metal felt solid in my hand, grounding me in a way I didn't fully understand. For a moment, I just stood there, staring at the knife as though it might explain itself.

Then the flashes came.

It started as a faint pressure at the back of my mind, like the memory of a dream I couldn't quite recall. Images flickered behind my eyes—disjointed and fragmented, like scenes from a broken film reel. A narrow alley, bathed in the dim glow of a streetlight. The sound of muffled screams, sharp and panicked, echoing against brick walls. The glint of the knife, its blade catching the light as it moved through the dark.

My hands tightened around the handle as the flashes grew more vivid. There was blood—dark, glistening, pooling on the ground. A shadowed figure slumped against the wall, their face blurred and indistinct. The sound of wet footsteps echoed in my ears, growing louder until they drowned out everything else.

I blinked, and the images were gone.

My chest heaved as I tried to steady my breathing. The knife was still in my hand, its blade as clean and sharp as ever. I set it on the desk, my fingers trembling slightly as I released it. It sat there, innocuous and unassuming, but I couldn't shake the feeling that it didn't belong there—or anywhere.

I pulled the chair out and sat down, my eyes fixed on the knife. The longer I stared at it, the more it seemed to fill the room, its presence overwhelming and intrusive. It wasn't just a tool or an object; it was a question, one I didn't have an answer to.

The muffled screams replayed in my mind, faint and distant, like an echo from another life. I tried to piece them together, to make sense of the fragments, but they slipped through my fingers like sand. Was it real? A memory? A dream? I couldn't tell anymore. All I knew was the weight of the knife, the feel of it in my hand, and the way it seemed to hold secrets I wasn't ready to uncover.

I sat there for what felt like hours, the knife and I locked in a silent standoff. The room grew darker as the sun dipped below the horizon, the shadows stretching long and thin across the floor. The fridge hummed softly in the background, its noise a steady counterpoint to the chaos in my head.

Eventually, I reached out and turned the knife slightly, aligning it perfectly with the edge of the desk. The action was small, insignificant, but it felt like an attempt to impose order on something that refused to be tamed.

The muffled screams faded, leaving only the faint metallic tang of blood lingering in my mind. I told myself it wasn't real, that it couldn't be real. But the knife gleamed under the dim light, its blade catching the faintest hint of red.

And I wasn't sure if it was the light or a memory.

Chapter 14: The Stranger Returns

The hallway light flickered again as I stepped outside my apartment. The faint buzzing sound it made had become part of the building's charm—or its warning, depending on how you looked at it. My door locked with a firm click, the sound louder than it needed to be in the silence. For a moment, I stood there, gripping the key in my pocket, feeling the familiar weight of unease pressing against me.

That's when I saw him.

The man was there again, standing further down the hallway, but closer than before. His presence hit me like a physical force. He was still, so still, as though frozen in time, his hat casting a shadow over his face. Even in the dim light, I could feel his eyes on me, watching with an intensity that made my skin crawl.

I didn't move. My fingers tightened around the key in my pocket, the sharp edges digging into my palm. He didn't speak, didn't shift, didn't do anything but exist in a way that felt wrong. The hallway felt longer than it should have, stretching endlessly between us, an expanse I didn't dare cross.

The air grew heavier, thick and oppressive, as though the building itself was holding its breath. My chest tightened, my pulse quickening as my thoughts spiraled into a cacophony of questions I couldn't answer. Who was he? Why was he here? And why did he feel so familiar?

The memory hit me before I could stop it: a struggle, the sensation of something slipping from my grasp, the weight of a body pressing against mine. It was fleeting, disjointed, like a dream half-remembered. But the feeling it left behind was sharp and undeniable—panic, raw and visceral, clawing its way to the surface.

I fumbled with the key, unlocking the door with shaking hands and slipping back inside. The door closed with a soft thud, the sound of the bolt sliding into place offering little comfort. My back pressed against the wood as I tried to steady my breathing, my chest rising and falling unevenly.

The knife was on the desk, exactly where I'd left it the night before. Its blade caught the dim light filtering through the blinds, gleaming faintly like it was waiting for me. I didn't hesitate this time. I crossed the room and picked it up, the weight of it grounding me in a way I didn't fully understand.

I sat in the chair by the window, the knife resting in my lap. My fingers traced the smooth surface of the handle, the cool metal sending a shiver up my spine. My breathing slowed, but the tension didn't leave my body. If anything, it coiled tighter, like a spring ready to snap.

The flashes came again, stronger now. A struggle in the dark, the sound of labored breathing, the sharp metallic clang of something hitting the ground. Hands grasping, clawing, pulling. A face—blurred, indistinct, but filled with fear.

I squeezed my eyes shut, trying to force the images away. They weren't real. They couldn't be. Just fragments of a mind stretched too thin, unraveling at the edges. But the more I tried to push them down, the more vivid they became. The alley, the footsteps, the faint metallic tang of blood—it all came rushing back, flooding my senses until I felt like I was drowning.

When I opened my eyes, the knife was still in my lap, its blade gleaming faintly in the dim light. My breathing was uneven, my chest tight with an ache I couldn't explain. I gripped the knife tighter, the coolness of the metal grounding me, keeping me tethered to the here and now.

The man's face lingered in my mind, his silhouette etched into the darkness like a shadow that refused to fade. He was just a neighbor, I told myself. A coincidence. Nothing more. But the memory of his stillness, the weight of his stare, said otherwise.

I turned the knife in my hands, the edge catching the light as I studied it. The flashes of the struggle felt too vivid, too real to be dismissed as imagination. But if they weren't real, then where had they come from? And if they were real...

My chest tightened as the thought trailed off, unfinished and unbearable. I set the knife back on the desk, its presence feeling heavier than ever. The hum of the fridge filled the silence, a low, steady rhythm that did nothing to ease the tension in the room.

I didn't sleep that night. I sat by the window, watching the shadows shift and stretch under the streetlights, the knife always within reach. The stranger's face haunted me, his presence looming larger with each passing hour. I told myself it was nothing, just my mind playing tricks, feeding off the weight of the unanswered questions.

But deep down, I wasn't sure if I believed that.

And I wasn't sure if I wanted to.

Chapter 15: A Quiet Goodbye

The day started like any other, wrapped in the suffocating routine I'd come to rely on. The office was dim and quiet, the buzz of fluorescent lights above blending seamlessly with the rhythm of typing and the occasional shuffle of papers. I sat at my desk, my fingers gliding over the keyboard in mechanical precision, filing data that would be forgotten the moment it was entered.

Karen's voice broke through the monotony. "You look...off today," she said, pausing by my cubicle with her usual cup of coffee in hand.

Her tone wasn't cruel, but the words hit me like a physical blow. Off. The word hung in the air, sharp and accusatory. Was it the circles under my eyes? The slouched posture I hadn't bothered to correct? The way my hands trembled slightly as I typed?

"I'm fine," I said, forcing a smile that felt as fragile as glass. "Just tired."

She shrugged, her attention already drifting elsewhere. "If you say so." The comment was casual, a throwaway observation, but it stuck like a thorn.

The rest of the day passed in a blur. Karen's words echoed in my mind, twisting and warping into something much larger than they were. You look off today. Off. Like I didn't belong here, like I didn't belong anywhere. Every glance from a coworker felt like confirmation, every laugh from across the room like it was directed at me.

By lunch, I couldn't focus. The numbers on my screen blurred together, refusing to align no matter how many times I recalculated. My breaths came short and fast, my chest tightening with a pressure I couldn't explain.

At 3:14 p.m., I stood up, grabbed my bag, and walked out. No explanation, no goodbye—just the sound of my footsteps echoing down the hallway as I left the building for the last time.

The walk home was surreal, the world around me muted and dreamlike. The city buzzed with its usual chaos—cars honking, pedestrians weaving through the streets—but it all felt distant, like watching a movie with the sound turned down. My legs moved on autopilot, one step after another, carrying me forward without direction.

By the time I reached my apartment, the weight of what I'd done finally hit me. I locked the door behind me, dropped my bag on the floor, and collapsed into the chair by the window. The fridge hummed softly in the background, indifferent as always.

I stared at my hands, the faint tremor still lingering in my fingers. What now? What was I supposed to do now? The thought spiraled, looping endlessly until I couldn't tell where it began or ended.

It was only when I got up to pour a glass of water that I noticed the stain.

A small, dark blotch on the cuff of my sleeve, barely noticeable unless you were looking for it. I froze, my hand hovering over the faucet as I studied the mark. It was deep red, smeared slightly at the edges, like it had been wiped against something.

Sauce, I told myself. It had to be sauce. But I hadn't eaten anything red today. Or yesterday.

The memory of the flashes returned: the alley, the knife, the muffled screams. My chest tightened as I rolled the fabric between my fingers, trying to convince myself it was nothing. A mistake. A coincidence. Something easily explained.

I turned on the faucet and let the water run cold before scrubbing at the stain, the fabric rough against my skin. The blotch faded slightly, but it didn't disappear. It clung stubbornly, a reminder I couldn't erase.

Back at the desk, the knife sat in its usual spot, its blade catching the dim light. I picked it up, turning it over in my hands, the weight grounding me in a way that felt both comforting and unnerving. The edge was as sharp as ever, unmarked, but my thoughts kept circling back to the stain.

What had I done? Or, more terrifyingly, what hadn't I done? The fragments of memory flickered in my mind like a broken film reel, too disjointed to make sense of.

I set the knife down carefully, aligning it perfectly with the edge of the desk. My breathing was uneven, my chest tight with the weight of questions I couldn't answer. The fridge hummed in the background, its rhythm steady and indifferent, a sharp contrast to the chaos in my mind.

That night, I lay in bed staring at the ceiling, the cracks forming patterns I couldn't unsee. The stain on my sleeve was still there, faint but persistent, a reminder I couldn't escape. I told myself it didn't matter, that it was just sauce, that I'd imagined the rest.

But deep down, I wasn't sure if I believed that.

And I wasn't sure if I wanted to.

Chapter 16: The Stain on the Floor

The morning felt heavier than it should have. The air in the apartment seemed denser, clinging to my skin and making it hard to breathe. The fridge hummed softly in the background, a low, constant noise that usually faded into white noise but today felt like a reprimand. The knife still sat on the desk, a sentinel over my disjointed thoughts, its blade catching the faint morning light.

As I shuffled toward the kitchen, my foot caught on something sticky. I froze, looking down to find a small, dark stain on the floor. It was irregular, its edges uneven, as though it had been hastily smeared. For a moment, I just stared at it, my chest tightening with an inexplicable sense of dread.

I crouched down, running my fingers over the mark. It was dry, tacky against my skin, and a deep reddish-brown color that made my stomach churn. Coffee, I told myself. It had to be coffee. But I didn't remember spilling any, and the texture felt...wrong.

My thoughts spiraled, the edges of my vision blurring as the flashes began. The alley came first, narrow and shadowed, lit only by the pale glow of a flickering streetlight. Then the muffled screams, sharp and panicked, filling the empty space with a sound that refused to fade. My hands, slick and trembling, clutching the knife as its blade gleamed in the dim light.

I snapped back to the present, gasping for breath. The stain was still there, dark and unyielding against the floor. I grabbed a rag from the counter and doused it in hot water, scrubbing at the mark with frantic determination. The fabric rubbed raw against my fingers as I pressed harder and harder, willing the stain to disappear.

"It's just coffee," I muttered aloud, my voice shaky and unconvincing. "It's just coffee."

The stain began to fade, smearing into smaller patches under the force of my scrubbing. But no matter how much I worked, traces of it lingered, clinging stubbornly to the floor like a secret that refused to be buried.

The flashes returned as I scrubbed, more vivid this time. The sound of footsteps echoed through the alley, quick and deliberate, matching the rhythm of my beating heart. A figure loomed in the shadows, their face blurred and indistinct, their body slumping against the wall as the knife moved in my hand.

I stopped, the rag slipping from my fingers. My chest heaved as I stared at the floor, the remnants of the stain glinting faintly in the morning light. My hands trembled, the phantom sensation of the knife's weight still lingering in my grip.

I stumbled back to the desk, collapsing into the chair as I tried to steady my breathing. The knife was still there, its blade untouched, its handle smooth and pristine. It couldn't have been real. None of it could have been real. Just fragments of a dream, a mind stretched too thin under the weight of too many unanswered questions.

But the stain didn't feel like a dream. It felt tangible, undeniable, like evidence of something I couldn't remember—or didn't want to.

I ran my fingers through my hair, the motion doing little to calm the storm in my head. The stain was gone now, scrubbed away to a faint shadow, but its presence lingered in the back of my mind like a whisper I couldn't quite hear.

That night, as I lay in bed, the flashes returned. The alley, the knife, the sound of something wet hitting the pavement. My hands, slick and trembling, reaching out for something—or someone—I couldn't see.

When I woke, the stain was still gone. But I couldn't shake the feeling that it had left something behind.

Chapter 17: The Distance Widens

The silence from my family was deafening. The text messages from my sisters had stopped completely. At first, I thought it was temporary, a pause in their endless stream of updates about their lives. But the days stretched into weeks, and the absence of their chatter settled over me like a heavy blanket.

Even my mother had grown quieter. The calls that used to come weekly dwindled to every other week, then monthly. Now, her name popped up on my screen only once in a while, her voicemails left untouched in a folder I didn't open. Each notification felt like a stone sinking deeper into my chest.

Her latest voicemail sat at the top of the list, its timestamp fresh, the little blue dot a persistent reminder of its presence. My thumb hovered over the play button, but I couldn't bring myself to listen. I imagined her voice, soft but tired, filled with that familiar blend of concern and frustration she reserved just for me.

"Are you okay?" she'd probably ask, her words hesitant. "I haven't heard from you in a while. We're worried about you."

Worried. That word carried too much weight. I closed the app, silencing the thought as I tossed the phone onto the desk. The knife glinted in the corner of my eye, its blade catching the dim light of the room. I hadn't touched it since the stain on the floor, but its presence felt larger now, more insistent.

The apartment felt emptier than usual that evening. The fridge hummed its indifferent tune, the light above the desk casting long shadows across the room. I tried to distract myself, picking up a book from the shelf only to set it down moments later. The words blurred together, unreadable, as my thoughts spiraled into the void left by my family's absence.

By the time I went to bed, the weight of the silence was unbearable. The cracks in the ceiling stared back at me, their jagged lines forming patterns I couldn't name. I closed my eyes, hoping sleep would come quickly, but it didn't. Instead, the dream began.

I was running.

The street was narrow, the walls of the buildings on either side closing in like a vice. My breath came in ragged gasps, the sound of my footsteps echoing against the brick. Ahead of me, a figure darted through the shadows, their movements frantic and uncoordinated.

Their screams pierced the air, sharp and raw, ricocheting off the walls and stabbing into my ears. It wasn't just fear—it was desperation, the kind that made your stomach twist and your legs falter. I didn't stop. I couldn't stop. My feet pounded against the pavement, faster and faster, closing the distance between us.

I could see them more clearly now. Their silhouette was trembling, their hands outstretched as they stumbled forward. I reached out, my fingers brushing against the fabric of their jacket. They screamed again, the sound reverberating in my skull, and I—

I woke with a start, my chest heaving, the sound of their screams still ringing in my ears. The room was dark, the faint glow of the streetlights outside casting pale patterns on the walls. I stared at the ceiling, trying to steady my breathing, but the dream clung to me, vivid and unrelenting.

The knife sat on the desk, its blade gleaming faintly in the moonlight. I turned away, pulling the blanket tighter around me as though that might shield me from the images replaying in my mind.

The figure. The screams. The chase.

I told myself it was just a dream, a manifestation of stress and exhaustion. But deep down, I wasn't sure if I believed that.

And deep down, I wasn't sure if I wanted to.

Chapter 18: The Notes Turn Dark

The notes had started as a way to organize my thoughts, to impose some semblance of order on the chaos that had become my life. At first, they were simple—reminders to pay bills, go to work, eat. But over time, they had begun to change.

It started subtly, the tone shifting from practical to something heavier. "Don't forget to pay rent" became "Don't fall behind again." "Go to work" turned into "You can't afford to miss this." I told myself it was just stress, that my own thoughts were bleeding into the words I wrote. But today, the note on the fridge stopped me cold.

"You can't escape this."

The handwriting was mine, the same jagged scrawl I'd seen a hundred times before. But I didn't remember writing it. I stared at the words, my chest tightening as though the paper itself was accusing me. The fridge hummed softly, indifferent to the weight of the message pinned to it.

I tore the note down, crumpling it in my fist. The sound of the paper compressing was louder than it should have been, echoing in the quiet of the apartment. I threw it into the trash, but even as it disappeared into the pile of discarded remnants, its presence lingered, like a splinter lodged deep under my skin.

The fridge stood empty now, the absence of the note leaving a blank, oppressive space. I grabbed a pen and a fresh scrap of paper, intending to replace it with something more practical. But my hand trembled as I wrote, the words refusing to take shape. Every attempt felt wrong, the lines jagged and uneven, as though my own mind was rebelling against the act.

I set the pen down, defeated.

The knife on the desk seemed brighter tonight, its blade gleaming faintly in the dim light of the room. I hadn't moved it in days, but it felt closer somehow, its presence heavier. I walked over and stared at it, the glint of the metal catching my eye like a spark in the dark. It looked...different. Sharper, cleaner, more alive.

My fingers hesitated over the handle, the familiar weight of it beckoning me. I picked it up, turning it over in my hands. The blade caught the light again, its edge seeming to shimmer with intent. It wasn't just a tool anymore—it was something more, something I couldn't name but felt deep in my chest.

The flashes came again.

An alley, narrow and suffocating. The sound of footsteps, quick and desperate. A scream, sharp and raw, slicing through the air. My hands gripping the knife, its blade slick and trembling as it moved through the dark. The smell of copper, thick and metallic, filling my nostrils as a shadowed figure slumped to the ground.

I blinked, and the images dissolved, leaving only the knife and the dim light of the apartment. My breathing was uneven, my chest tight with the weight of questions I couldn't answer. I set the knife down carefully, aligning it perfectly with the edge of the desk.

The fridge hummed behind me, its sound steady and unchanging. I glanced at the empty space where the note had been, the faint smudge of adhesive still clinging to the surface. I thought about replacing it, about writing something simple, something hopeful. But the pen felt heavy in my hand, the paper resisting every word I tried to write.

The blankness of the fridge mirrored the blankness in my mind, a void I couldn't seem to fill. The knife gleamed in the corner of my eye, its presence unrelenting, its purpose undefined.

And in the silence of the apartment, I thought I heard the faint echo of footsteps, growing louder with every breath.

Chapter 19: Routines Become Rituals

The mornings blurred into afternoons, and the afternoons slipped into nights, each day a replica of the one before. My routines had always been a way to maintain control, to keep the chaos at bay. But lately, they felt less like habits and more like rituals—actions performed with a weight I couldn't explain.

Everything had its place. Everything had its order. I aligned the pens on my desk in perfect rows, each one equidistant from the next. The books on the shelf were sorted not just by genre but by height and thickness, their spines forming an unbroken line. I counted the steps from the bed to the kitchen and back again, adjusting my stride to ensure the number was always the same.

And then there was the knife.

I hadn't touched it in days, not since that night when the stain on the floor refused to fade from my thoughts. But tonight, its presence felt unavoidable, pulling at me like a magnet. I picked it up, the familiar weight grounding me, and walked to the kitchen.

The sharpening stone was something I'd bought years ago and never used until now. It sat in the back of the drawer, forgotten, until the knife demanded its attention. I set the blade against the stone, angling it carefully as I began to slide it back and forth, the rhythmic shhhk-shhhk filling the silence of the apartment.

As I worked, my mind began to wander. The sound of the blade against the stone faded, replaced by muffled echoes that didn't belong. Footsteps, quick and uneven, echoed through the recesses of my memory. The smell of copper, sharp and metallic, filled my nostrils. My hands moved faster, the blade gliding over the stone with a precision that felt automatic, almost instinctual.

The flashes came next, stronger and more vivid than before. The alley was dark, its walls pressing in on me as I ran. My breath came in gasps, each step heavy with the weight of something I couldn't name. A figure stumbled ahead of me, their shadow stretching long and thin under the flickering streetlight.

The knife was in my hand, its blade slick and trembling. A cry pierced the air, sharp and desperate, cutting through the noise of my pounding heart. I raised the knife, its edge gleaming in the dim light, and—

I stopped, my chest heaving as I stared down at the knife. The blade was sharper now, its edge smooth and flawless, reflecting the dim light of the kitchen. I ran my thumb along the edge, careful not to press too hard. The metal was cold, almost biting, as though it held a life of its own.

Had the knife always been this sharp? I couldn't remember. My mind replayed the image of the blade moving through the alley, its edge catching the faint glow of the streetlight. It felt real, too real to be dismissed as imagination. But it couldn't be real. Could it?

I set the knife down carefully, aligning it with the edge of the counter. The sharpening stone sat beside it, a faint trace of metal dust glinting under the light. My hands trembled as I wiped them on a towel, the friction grounding me, pulling me back to the present.

The fridge hummed softly behind me, its sound steady and indifferent. The routine was supposed to bring comfort, to impose order on the chaos. But tonight, it felt like the chaos had seeped into the routine, twisting it into something darker.

I stared at the knife, its blade gleaming with a purpose I didn't understand. The flashes lingered at the edges of my mind, fragmented and incomplete, their pieces refusing to fit together. I told myself it wasn't real, that it couldn't be real. But the knife gleamed, sharp and unyielding, as though it knew something I didn't.

That night, as I lay in bed, I couldn't stop thinking about the knife. The weight of it, the sharpness of its edge, the way it had felt in my hand. My routines had always been a sanctuary, a way to make sense of the world. But now, they felt like a trap, binding me to a purpose I couldn't name.

And in the quiet darkness of the apartment, the faint sound of footsteps echoed in my mind, growing louder with every passing moment.

Chapter 20: The Stranger's Presence

The hallway light buzzed faintly, its flicker casting uneven shadows across the scuffed linoleum floor. I hesitated before stepping out, the door creaking as I opened it. The hallway was quiet, empty save for the faint hum of the elevator at the far end. I told myself it was just another day, another mundane trip down these familiar corridors.

But then I saw him.

He was standing closer this time, only a few feet from my door, his presence a solid weight in the narrow space. His hat was tilted low, obscuring most of his face, but his posture was rigid, his hands tucked into the pockets of a heavy coat. He didn't move as I stepped out. He just stared.

"Excuse me," I mumbled, trying to sidestep him, but he shifted, blocking my path.

"You think you can just keep going?" His voice was low, rough, and it hit me like a slap. "Like nothing happened?"

I froze, my chest tightening as I met his gaze. His eyes were dark, unreadable, but there was something in them—something accusing, something sharp. My mouth opened, but no words came out.

"What are you talking about?" I managed finally, my voice unsteady.

"You know damn well what I'm talking about," he said, stepping closer. The faint scent of cigarettes clung to his coat, mingling with the stale air of the hallway. "I've seen you. I've seen what you've done."

The words hit me like a physical blow. My mind raced, fragments of memory flashing behind my eyes: the alley, the knife, the muffled screams. Blood on my hands, slick and warm, dripping onto the pavement. I shook my head, trying to force the images away.

"You're mistaken," I said, my voice shaking. "I haven't... I haven't done anything."

He laughed, a harsh, bitter sound that echoed through the empty hallway. "Is that what you tell yourself? That it's all in your head?" He leaned in closer, his face inches from mine. "You're not as innocent as you think."

My breath quickened. The flashes came stronger now, more vivid: the glint of the knife, the sound of footsteps, the metallic tang of blood in the air. I took a step back, my hand fumbling for the door handle.

"I don't know what you're talking about," I said, the words coming out too fast, too defensive.

He tilted his head, his eyes narrowing. "Keep lying to yourself, then. But you can't hide from the truth forever." His voice was calm now, almost pitying. "It always finds you."

I turned and slipped back into the apartment, slamming the door shut behind me. My hands trembled as I locked it, once, twice, the sound of the bolt sliding into place barely audible over the pounding of my heart. I leaned against the door, my chest heaving as I tried to steady my breathing.

The apartment felt too small, the walls pressing in as the man's words echoed in my mind. I've seen you. I've seen what you've done. My eyes darted to the desk, to the knife sitting there in its usual place. Its blade gleamed faintly in the dim light, catching my gaze like it had something to say.

I stumbled toward the desk, my legs unsteady, and picked up the knife. The weight of it felt heavier now, more real. The flashes came again: shadows stretching long and thin under a flickering streetlight, a figure slumping against the wall, the sound of something wet hitting the ground.

I gripped the knife tighter, my knuckles white as I stared at it. The man's voice rang in my ears, his accusations blending with the fragmented memories I couldn't piece together. Was he right? Had I done something—something I couldn't remember, or didn't want to?

I set the knife down carefully, its blade catching the faint glow of the desk lamp. My breathing slowed, but the tension in my chest didn't ease. I glanced at the door, the locks standing between me and the man in the hallway. He was gone now, his presence replaced by the silence of the building.

But his words lingered, carving themselves into my thoughts.

And as I sat there, staring at the knife, I couldn't shake the feeling that he wasn't entirely wrong.

Chapter 21: The Final Debt

The envelope arrived in the usual stack of mail, nestled innocuously between a coupon booklet and a flier for a pizza place I'd never tried. Its weight felt heavier than the others, though, as if it carried something far more significant than its modest size suggested. The bold red letters across the top confirmed it: FINAL NOTICE.

I sat at the desk, the unopened envelope in my hand. The hum of the fridge was louder today, filling the room with a low, persistent buzz that seemed to amplify the silence around it. My fingers trembled as I peeled the flap open, the faint tear of the paper almost deafening in the stillness.

The number at the bottom of the page was a punch to the gut. It wasn't just a bill—it was a sentence, a declaration of everything I'd failed to manage, failed to control. $15,932.76. Past due. Payable immediately. My eyes scanned the rest of the letter, but the words blurred together, their meaning drowned out by the sheer weight of that number.

It was too much. Too big. Too final.

My hands shook as I set the notice on the desk, its presence looming over me like a shadow. The knife lay nearby, its blade gleaming faintly in the dim light. The two objects sat side by side, stark and silent, as though waiting for me to make a decision.

I reached for a scrap of paper, the pen trembling in my grip. The words came haltingly, each one dragging itself out like it didn't want to be written.

"I'm sorry."

I stared at the words, their simplicity mocking me. Sorry for what? For failing? For forgetting? For not knowing the difference between reality and whatever it was that clawed at the edges of my mind? The flashes came again, sharp and intrusive: the alley, the blood, the muffled screams.

My hand moved almost unconsciously, adding another line.

"I didn't mean to..."

I stopped. Didn't mean to what? The question hung in the air, unanswered and unanswerable. The memories were too fragmented, too distorted, their pieces refusing to fit together. I couldn't confess to something I wasn't sure was real.

I crumpled the paper, tossing it into the trash with a force that made the bag rustle loudly in the otherwise silent room. The apology felt hollow, a shadow of something I couldn't fully grasp. My eyes drifted back to the notice, its bold red lettering staring back at me like a challenge.

I folded it carefully, the creases sharp and deliberate, and placed it next to the knife. The two objects seemed to belong together now, their presence filling the space with a gravity I couldn't ignore.

The knife's blade caught the faint glow of the desk lamp, its edge shimmering with a quiet menace. My fingers hovered over the handle, but I didn't pick it up. Not yet.

The fridge hummed on, indifferent to the weight of the moment. I sat back in the chair, my chest tight with the pressure of everything I couldn't name. The debt notice, the knife, the flashes—they all blurred together into a singular weight, pressing down on me until I could barely breathe.

For a moment, I thought about writing another note, something more definitive, something that could explain everything I couldn't. But what was there to explain? I wasn't even sure what was real anymore. The memories, the accusations, the flashes of violence—they felt too vivid to be imagined, yet too fragmented to be trusted.

The knife gleamed, its blade sharp and unforgiving. The folded notice sat beside it, a quiet reminder of the life I was failing to hold together.

I leaned back, closing my eyes, and let the hum of the fridge fill the silence.

Chapter 22: A Reflection That Lies

The bathroom mirror was cracked at the corner, a jagged line that spidered out across the glass like a web. It had been like that when I moved in, but tonight it seemed sharper, its edges glinting under the dim yellow light. I leaned closer, staring at the face that stared back at me, trying to reconcile what I saw with what I felt.

It wasn't me—not entirely. The man in the mirror looked calm, almost smug, his eyes steady and unyielding. There was no tremor in his hands, no tension in his jaw. His expression was serene, controlled, as though he'd just finished solving a puzzle only he could understand.

I tilted my head, and so did he, but the movement felt off, delayed by a fraction of a second. My breath hitched, my chest tightening as I stepped closer, the faint outline of my reflection distorting along the crack in the glass. I studied him—studied me—but the more I looked, the less I recognized.

The reflection's lips twitched, almost imperceptibly, as though it were about to speak. I froze, the air in the bathroom became suffocating. My own voice broke the silence, barely a whisper.

"If I did it... wouldn't I know?"

The words hung in the air, sharp and unanswered. The reflection didn't move, didn't react. It just stared back at me, its calmness unwavering, its gaze boring into mine with a weight I couldn't escape.

The flashes came again, unbidden and intrusive. The knife in my hand, slick with something warm. The alley, narrow and shadowed. A figure slumped against the wall, their face blurred and indistinct. The sound of wet footsteps, quick and deliberate, echoing through the dark.

I gripped the edge of the sink, my knuckles white as the images faded. The reflection didn't change. It remained calm, composed, its eyes steady as it watched me fall apart.

"Tell me," I whispered, my voice trembling. "If I did it, wouldn't I know?"

The reflection said nothing. Its silence was louder than any answer it could have given, more damning than any accusation. I turned the faucet on, the rush of cold water filling the room and drowning out the sound of my own breathing.

I splashed my face, the icy shock grounding me, pulling me back to the present. When I looked up, the reflection was still there, unchanged. But something in its eyes had shifted, something I couldn't name. It was subtle, almost imperceptible, but it left a chill crawling up my spine.

I left the bathroom without turning off the light. The hum of the fridge greeted me as I stepped into the main room, its steady rhythm a faint comfort against the weight in my chest. The knife sat on the desk, its blade shining faintly beside the folded debt notice.

I sat down, staring at the knife, my mind circling back to the reflection. The face in the mirror, calm and unyielding, its silence speaking louder than any words ever could.

If I did it... wouldn't I know?

The question lingered, unanswered, as the knife glinted under the dim light, sharp and waiting.

Chapter 23: The Final Note

The pen felt impossibly heavy in my hand as I stared at the blank scrap of paper. The words swirled in my mind, sharp and clear, but putting them down felt like crossing a line I wasn't sure I was ready to cross. My fingers trembled as the pen hovered above the page, the silence of the apartment pressing in on me like a physical weight.

The knife sat on the desk, its blade glowed faintly in the dim light. It had been a presence in my life for so long now, a constant companion I couldn't seem to part with. Tonight, though, it felt different—closer, heavier, more alive.

The words finally came, dragging themselves out like reluctant confessions.

"This ends tonight."

I stared at the note, the ink smudging slightly under my fingers as I set the pen down. The finality of the words sent a shiver through me, their simplicity more powerful than I'd anticipated. There was no ambiguity here, no room for second-guessing. It was a decision, a declaration, an end.

My eyes drifted to the knife. Its presence was magnetic, pulling at me with an intensity that made my chest tighten. I reached for it, my fingers wrapping around the handle with a familiarity that felt both comforting and unsettling.

It was heavier than I remembered, its weight grounding me, anchoring me to the moment. The blade caught the light, its edge sharp and unyielding, reflecting the faint glow of the desk lamp. I turned it over in my hand, feeling the smoothness of the handle, the coldness of the metal.

For a moment, I just sat there, staring at the knife, my mind circling back to the same question it had been asking for weeks.

Is this the first time I've held it with purpose? Or the hundredth?

The flashes returned, more vivid than ever. The alley, the shadows, the sound of footsteps quick and desperate. The knife in my hand, slick and trembling. A figure slumped against the wall, their face blurred but their fear palpable. The smell of copper, thick and metallic, filling the air.

The images felt real—too real. But were they memories? Or something else entirely? My chest tightened as the question twisted itself into a knot I couldn't untangle.

I set the knife down for a moment, aligning it perfectly with the edge of the desk. The note sat beside it, the ink unyielding against the paper. The two objects seemed to belong together now, their presence filling the space with a gravity I couldn't ignore.

The fridge hummed softly in the background, its steady rhythm a sharp contrast to the chaos in my mind. I stared at the note, the words searing themselves into my thoughts: This ends tonight.

The knife's blade catching the faintest hint of red under the dim light. I told myself it was just a trick of the light, that my mind was playing games with me. But the weight of the knife in my hand felt too familiar, too certain.

I picked it up again, and as I turned it over in my hands, it felt like it belonged there, like it had always belonged there. My breaths came slow and uneven, the weight of the moment pressing down on me with a force I couldn't escape.

Is this the first time? Or the hundredth?

The question lingered, unanswered, as I stared at the knife and the note, their presence filling the room with an unbearable stillness.

Chapter 24: The Weight of the Knife

The knife was colder than I expected, its blade glinting faintly under the pale light of the desk lamp. I ran my fingers along the handle, tracing its contours, feeling the smoothness of the metal. Its weight felt heavier than before, though whether that was real or imagined, I couldn't say.

I turned it over in my hands, the edge catching the light, sharp and unyielding. It was familiar now, almost comforting, like an old friend I hadn't realized I'd been missing. But tonight, the comfort was laced with something else, something heavier.

The memories came in fragments, disjointed and incomplete, flashing behind my eyes as though summoned by the blade itself. The alley, the muffled screams, the warm slickness of blood on my hands. The sound of wet footsteps echoing against the brick walls, the faint metallic tang in the air. Each image felt like a puzzle piece that refused to fit, their edges jagged and sharp.

I gripped the knife tighter, the handle pressing into my palm as I tried to sort through the chaos in my mind. Were these memories? Dreams? Something in between? The more I thought about it, the less certain I became. But the feelings they left behind—fear, guilt, resignation—were undeniable.

I positioned the blade against my wrist, the cold steel biting into my skin. My hand trembled slightly as I pressed down, the sharpness of the edge sending a faint shiver up my arm. The sensation was grounding, anchoring me to the moment, pulling me out of the haze of uncertainty.

The flashes came again, stronger now. The alley stretched out before me, its walls closing in like a vice. The knife was in my hand, its blade glinting as it moved through the shadows. A scream pierced the air, raw and desperate, slicing through the silence like a blade through flesh.

I blinked, and the images faded, leaving only the faint hum of the fridge and the weight of the knife in my hand. My chest hurt as I stared at the blade, the edge pressing into my skin but not breaking it. The reflection from the desk lamp danced along the surface, creating patterns that seemed almost alive.

The memories—if they were memories—lingered at the edges of my mind, taunting me with their incompleteness. Had it happened? Had I done those things? Or was my mind playing tricks on me, twisting dreams into something more sinister?

I closed my eyes, the blade still resting against my wrist. The silence of the apartment pressed in around me, heavy and oppressive. My breathing slowed, the tension in my chest easing as I focused on the weight of the knife, the coolness of the metal, the faint sting of its edge.

This ends tonight.

The words from the note echoed in my mind, their finality settling over me like a blanket. I opened my eyes, staring down at the blade, its presence steady and unrelenting. My grip tightened, the metal cool in my hand.

The blade pressed into my skin, the pressure building as I leaned into it. My chest felt lighter now, the weight of the decision lifting as I gave myself over to the moment.

Chapter 25: A Room in Silence

The apartment was quiet, the kind of quiet that swallowed everything whole. The hum of the fridge, the faint creak of the walls—they were still there, but they felt distant, muffled, as if the air had thickened and muted the world around me. The desk lamp cast a weak glow, its light barely reaching the corners of the room.

I sat in the chair, the knife resting in my hand, its weight steady and familiar. The blade glinted faintly, a sliver of silver cutting through the darkness. My eyes traced its edge, sharp and unrelenting, as my mind wandered back to the fragments of memory that refused to leave me.

The alley came first, its narrow walls closing in like a cage. The sound of footsteps echoed, quick and frantic, chasing me—or perhaps being chased. A scream followed, piercing and desperate, cutting through the air like a blade. My hands were slick with something warm, the knife trembling in my grasp as the figure in front of me crumpled to the ground.

The flashes blurred, their edges jagged and incomplete, leaving behind only sensations. The smell of copper, the weight of the knife, the pressure in my chest. I tried to piece them together, to make sense of what they meant, but the harder I tried, the more they slipped away.

I stared at the knife, its edge catching the dim light. It felt like the only thing in the room that was real, the only thing that hadn't blurred into abstraction. My grip tightened around the handle as I leaned back in the chair, the wood creaking softly under my weight.

The truth. Did it matter anymore? Whether the memories were real or imagined, whether the flashes were dreams or something darker—did it change anything? The weight in my chest, the ache in my head, the emptiness in the pit of my stomach—they were all real enough.

I closed my eyes, letting the silence wash over me. The fragments played behind my eyelids like a broken film reel, the images disjointed but relentless. The knife in my hand, the blood on the ground, the figure slumped against the wall. The flashes didn't answer my questions. They only raised more.

When I opened my eyes, the knife was still there, steady and waiting. My thumb ran along the edge, the sharpness biting into my skin without breaking it. The coolness of the metal sent a shiver up my spine, grounding me in the moment.

The room felt smaller now, the walls pressing in like the alley in my memories. My breathing slowed as I lifted the knife, its blade catching the light one last time. My chest felt lighter, the tension easing as I let go of the questions, the doubts, the endless cycle of what-ifs.

The truth didn't matter. Not anymore.

The knife moved, its edge pressing into my skin with purpose.

Chapter 26: The Edge of the Blade

The knife's edge kissed my skin, its cold bite sending a shiver through me. For a moment, there was only the pressure, sharp and unyielding, like the world narrowing down to a single point of contact. Then, the blade pressed deeper, slicing through with an ease that felt both shocking and inevitable.

The first sensation was warmth. A rush of heat spread across my wrist, pooling quickly, its texture was unrelenting. The vivid crimson contrasted starkly with the pale glow of the desk lamp, the fluid catching the light as it spilled onto the wood below. The sound was faint, a quiet patter like raindrops on a roof, almost soothing in its rhythm.

A sharp sting followed, radiating out from the cut like ripples in water. It wasn't the unbearable pain I'd imagined—more like an insistent ache, a reminder of the act itself. Blood continued to flow, painting my hand, the desk, the floor.

Relief came next, soft and unexpected. It washed over me in waves, loosening the knots in my chest, lightening the weight in my head. The tension that had gripped me for weeks, months, maybe years, began to fade, replaced by a strange, quiet calm. My body felt heavy, anchored to the chair, but my mind was lighter, unburdened.

The flashes came again, but this time, they were softer, less jagged. The alley, the knife, the figure in the shadows—they played out like scenes from a distant dream, detached and surreal. The muffled screams were quieter now, their sharp edges dulled by the haze settling over me.

A flicker of uncertainty cut through the calm, sharp as the blade itself. My eyes drifted to the blood pooling on the desk, the contrast of red against the pale wood. It felt surreal, like looking at someone else's hand, someone else's life. The question lingered at the edges of my mind, faint but insistent.

Is this right? Is this enough?

The knife slipped from my grasp, clattering softly against the desk. My hand felt lighter without it, the weight of the blade replaced by the warmth of the blood. I leaned back in the chair, my breaths slowing as my body adjusted to the loss.

The room was quiet, save for the faint hum of the fridge and the rhythmic patter of blood on the floor. The relief was still there, but it was tinged with something else now—a faint unease, a whisper of doubt that refused to be silenced.

The warmth spread further, the pool growing wider, reaching the edges of the desk. I closed my eyes, the weight of the moment pressing against me as the stillness settled in.

For the first time in what felt like forever, I didn't try to fight it.

Chapter 27: A Life Unseen

The world was softening around the edges, colors fading into muted tones as the heaviness in my limbs spread. The warmth from the cut felt distant now, its presence dulled as my body began to surrender to the pull of the moment. The knife sat on the desk, its blade streaked with red, the reflection of the dim light fractured in its sheen.

My head lolled back against the chair, and my thoughts began to drift, unmoored and scattered, as though my mind were flipping through the pages of a life that barely felt like mine. Memories rose and fell like the tide, each one lingering for a moment before being swallowed.

Isolation was the first. The apartment, with its faint hum of the fridge and the way the walls seemed to close in a little more each day. The silence that followed me home, that greeted me every morning, that filled the spaces where laughter or conversation might have been. It wasn't loneliness exactly—it was something deeper, heavier. A sense of being apart from everything, of existing on the edges of a world I couldn't quite reach.

Debt followed close behind, its weight pressing against me even now. The envelopes with their final notices, the numbers that refused to add up no matter how many times I recalculated. The bills I couldn't pay, the jobs I couldn't keep, the constant, gnawing reminder that I was always falling behind.

And, the flashes. The alley, the shadows, the muffled screams. The blood on my hands, the knife in my grasp. Were they memories, or dreams? Real, or imagined? The uncertainty gnawed at me, its edges jagged and sharp, as though my own mind were trying to swallow itself whole.

My breaths came slower now, each one shallower than the last. The pool of blood on the desk reflected the faint glow of the lamp, its surface rippling faintly with the vibration of the fridge. The warmth that had felt so visceral before was fading now, replaced by a growing coldness that crept up my arms and into my chest.

The question rose unbidden, soft but insistent: Was peace ever possible?

I thought of the notes on the fridge, the knife on the desk, the faces of my family that had blurred over time. I thought of the debt, the routines, the fragments of a life that had never quite come together. The possibility of peace felt like something I'd dreamed of once, a concept now too far removed from reality to ever take shape.

The room grew dimmer, the light fading as though the apartment itself were retreating. My eyelids feel heavy, my vision is narrowing to a single point before slipping into darkness. The silence pressed in, deeper now, more complete, wrapping around me like a blanket.

As the final flickers of consciousness ebbed away, I wondered if the relief I'd felt moments ago was peace, or if peace was just another thing I'd imagined, another fragment of a life unseen.

And then..

Chapter 28: Finding Peace

The edges of the world blurred like watercolors left in the rain, everything softening, melting into itself. My body felt weightless, untethered, as though I were drifting somewhere just beyond the reach of the room.

My vision narrowed, tunneling toward the dim light of the desk lamp. The knife sat there, still and steady, its blade streaked with red, a stark reminder of what I'd done—or perhaps of who I'd always been. The pool of blood spread further, a quiet ripple across the surface of the desk, reflecting fractured images I couldn't quite make out.

The memories came in flashes now, softer than before, their jagged edges smoothed by the haze settling over me. The alley, the shadows, the muffled cries—they flickered like an old film reel, skipping frames, their details indistinct. The knife glinted in my hand, its weight familiar, its purpose unclear.

Were they real? Or just fragments of a mind stretched too thin, twisting dreams into something darker? The question circled endlessly, its answer slipping further from reach with each passing moment.

I blinked slowly, the motion heavy, my eyelids refusing to lift again. The silence in the room deepened, wrapping around me like a cocoon. The warmth of the blood had faded, replaced by a creeping cold that seeped into my skin, settling deep in my bones.

My final thought surfaced gently, like the last ripple in a still pond: I'll never know.

I let it go, the words dissolving into the quiet that overtook me, filling every corner of my mind until there was nothing left.

And then, silence.

Chapter 29: The Final Act

The world was soft now, a place without sharp edges or harsh lines. Everything seemed to blend together—the dim glow of the desk lamp, the faint hum of the fridge, the cool air settling over my skin. Time stretched and folded in on itself, leaving me suspended somewhere between clarity and haze.

The room felt distant, like a place I'd visited once in a dream, its details slipping through my fingers the harder I tried to hold onto them. The knife, the blood, the note—they were still there, but their weight had lessened, their presence dulled by the fog enveloping me.

My thoughts wandered, untethered, flickering between moments like leaves caught in the wind. I saw myself walking down the hallway, passing strangers whose faces blurred into shadows. I saw the alley, the glint of the knife, the muffled sound of footsteps on wet pavement. The memories—or were they imaginings?—felt both vivid and unreal, their edges shimmering like heat waves.

The sensation of the knife pressing into my skin returned, fleeting and faint, as though it were happening to someone else. I could again feel the warmth of the blood pooling around me, its texture thick and unyielding, but the discomfort was gone now, replaced by a strange, quiet acceptance.

Questions rose unbidden, swirling in my mind without answers. Had it been real? The flashes of violence, the stranger in the hallway, the weight of guilt pressing down on me for weeks—were they pieces of a truth I couldn't face, or fragments of a mind unraveling under its own weight?

The question lingered, hanging in the air like smoke, but I found I didn't need the answer. Maybe I never had.

The room shifted, its boundaries fading further as the haze deepened. The hum of the fridge became softer, more rhythmic, like a heartbeat slowing to a whisper. The light from the desk lamp seemed to pulse faintly, its glow stretching and retreating as though it were breathing. I closed my eyes, and the darkness behind my eyelids felt vast, endless, like stepping into a void.

For a moment, I thought of the knife—the sharpness of its blade, the weight of it in my hand, the way it had felt like both a tool and a question. But the thought drifted away, carried off by the fog, leaving only the faint echo of its presence.

As the silence deepened, a final thought surfaced, quiet and unassuming, like the last ember of a dying fire: Maybe it doesn't matter anymore.

And with that, the fog took everything else.

Chapter 30: Fade to Black

The stillness wrapped around me like a blanket, soft and infinite. The hum of the fridge had faded completely, its absence leaving a silence so deep it felt like the apartment itself had ceased to exist. The light of the desk lamp no longer reached me. Instead, there was only darkness, warm and enveloping, stretching endlessly in every direction.

I tried to open my eyes, but they stayed closed, heavy and unresponsive. It didn't matter. I wasn't sure there was anything left to see. The world I had known—the apartment, the knife, the fragments of memories—felt distant now, like echoes from a life that had belonged to someone else.

The weight in my chest eased further, replaced by a lightness I hadn't known was possible. My thoughts drifted like leaves on a still pond, each one slower and quieter than the last. There was no pain, no guilt, no questions demanding answers.

Just the quiet. Endless and complete.

I wasn't sure if I was floating or falling. There was no direction, no gravity, only the sensation of being carried, cradled by the silence. The edges of my mind blurred, my thoughts unraveling into the void, each one fading before it could fully take shape.

Time no longer mattered. I couldn't say if seconds or hours passed, but the absence of measurement felt freeing, like stepping outside of a cage I hadn't realized I was in. The knife, the blood, the memories—they all slipped away, their weight no longer pressing against me.

The silence deepened, becoming more than an absence of sound. It was a presence, vast and steady, filling every corner of my being. It wasn't the void I had feared—it was something gentler, something almost kind.

The final thought came, soft and certain, rising from somewhere deep within: The quiet I'd been searching for was here, real or not.

Don't miss out!

Visit the website below and you can sign up to receive emails whenever Johnny Gee publishes a new book. There's no charge and no obligation.

https://books2read.com/r/B-A-NXELC-QIUIF

BOOKS 2 READ

Connecting independent readers to independent writers.

Also by Johnny Gee

Milton Keynes UK
Ingram Content Group UK Ltd.
UKHW030149051224
452010UK00001B/25